To Réglisse, Rasta, and Calypso.

B.V.

minedition

North American edition published 2019 by Michael Neugebauer Publishing Ltd. Hong Kong

Text copyright © 2019 Bernard Villiot
Illustrations copyright © 2019 Antoine Guilloppé
English text adaption by Kathryn Bishop
Rights arranged with "minedition" Rights and Licensing AG, Zurich, Switzerland.

Michael Neugebauer Publishing Ltd.,
Unit 28, 5/F, Metro Centre, Phase 2, No.21 Lam Hing Street, Kowloon Bay, Kowloon, Hong Kong
Phone: +852 2807 1711, e-mail: info@minedition.com
This book was printed in January 2019 at L.Rex Ltd
3/F., Blue Box Factory Building, 25 Hing Wo Street, Tin Wan, Aberdeen, Hong Kong, China
Typesetting in RitaSmith.
Library of Congress Cataloging-in-Publication Data available upon request.

ISBN 978-988-8341-86-3
10 9 8 7 6 5 4 3 2 1
First Impression

For more information please visit our website: www.minedition.com

Mephisto

BERNARD VILLIOT · ANTOINE GUILLOPPÉ

minedition

There was a time when I only went out at night,
once parents put their little ones to bed.

I was avoided to ward off bad luck.

I was considered a jinx, unlucky,
and who knows what else.

Nobody wanted to cross my path
because it was said that the devil
hid under my fur.

I was a cursed cat,
a cursed black cat,

Black as night,
black as soot,
black as trouble.

And so, I was saddled with a gloomy name:

Mephisto

I would have liked a nicer name,
one you'd give to a hardy tomcat

like the ones that cuddle in front of a fire,
stretched out on someone's knees.

But as far as people were concerned
I was worthless.

I was considered a thief or a fighter;
I was up to no good.

If I was out at night stealing something to eat here and there,
it was because moving around at night kept me warm.

If I lashed out with my claws,
it was because someone had scared me.

A little bit of love would have gone a long way in taming me.

I had no master nor a place to call my own.
All I had were the roofs to keep me dry.

I had no treats.
All I had were rats and mice to keep my stomach full.

You might say that I was free.
But what good is that if nobody wants you?

One night, I ran away.

I ran away from the city,
from people and their stupidity.

I ran away from their taunting
and their cruelty.

Nobody was worried about me.

Nobody came looking for me.

I walked for six whole days
without stopping very much,
so that I could find a more pleasant place to live

where nobody would throw rocks and insults at me,
where nobody would call attention to
my color or the way I moved.

When the sun started to go down,
guided by the sound of cowbells,
I climbed the steep path of a hill.

I had hoped to find the place
I'd always dreamed of settling down there,
the sole feline amongst the bovines.

But I had to give that idea up,
driven away as I was by the hawthorn bush's needles.

And then one morning I finally found what I was looking for,
where the honeysuckle and juniper bushes met,
a piece of heaven that I'd been looking for.

An expanse of flowers and greenery
far from the commotion and cars.

A horizon of sky and nature
far from disorder and misadventures.

I made this place my garden in exile
so that I could live a happy life.

And now I could mew,
hunt and gambol with complete freedom.

I would spend whole days
frolicking in the perfumed ditches and thickets.

I teased butterflies on the poppy-dappled slopes
and tasted the sweet treat of voles and field mice.

Nasty canines sometimes sought me out to quarrel,
but nothing like the cruelty given to me by people.

These were just little scuffles.

In short, I found peace.

When night fell, I'd fall asleep under the skies,
and was haunted by memories of the past.

My dreams were constantly being interrupted.

I dreamed that I was satisfied, and purring near a wood stove,
when suddenly, a shadow would appear to chase me away.

I dreamed that I was under a beauty's balcony, my recital of
meows a cacophony of brilliance.

And then suddenly, someone yelled "silence!" while throwing a
slipper or even a shoe at me.

Fear took hold of me in the middle of the night.
It was the same each time, striking me as I slept.

When I awoke, I moved around to forget,
to escape the painful memories of my thoughts.

First I would groom my fur,
then some stretching so that I could stay alert and spry.

Through the weeks and months that followed
I learned how to live without fear or anxiety.

There were nights of storms
where thunder and lightning raged in the sky.

But it was nothing to be afraid of.

I lived this way, far from people

through a summer,
through an autumn.

But when the winter's wind froze the end of my nose,
I started to miss the roofs and the attics that were heated by
chimney pipes.

Despite my exile, I was still a city cat.

So I returned with hesitation,
my hair covered in frost.

Who could fear the sinister cat
who was currently all white?

When I rounded a corner in the city, someone recognized me.

"Mephisto," he cried.
"Mephisto has come back!"

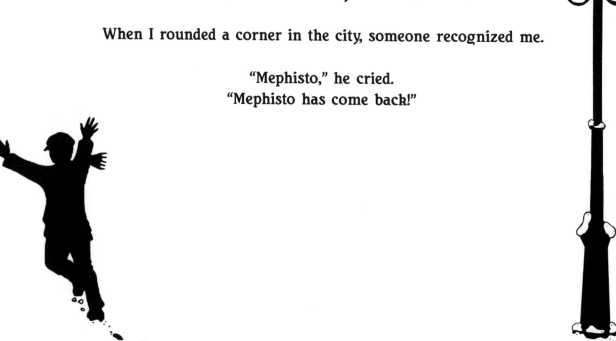

Others saw me and came closer.
Wary, I reminded them of my claws and my teeth.

But nobody chased me that day.

They all complimented me
and covered me in caresses.

Had people changed so much
over a single summer?

Their kindness and their attention
let me know that things weren't going well.

The rats and the mice had taken a foothold
in their homes after I'd left.

And their large tomcats who had been so well
fed did not care that the people were being overrun.

I was no longer unlucky,
I was a blessing.

They prayed, and they begged.

They promised me mountains and marvels
if I would just make the mice and the rats go away,
which I did within the hour.

I stalked them, pawed at them, fumbled around
with them and ran them off without stopping.

When someone's cellar had been liberated of these intruders,
I immediately started working on the attic of another.

And in less time than it took to speak,
I made everyone smile.

A hero, I was offered
a thousand favors in return.

But I refused these privileges.

Why, you ask?
To keep my freedom, of course.

Today, I meow and purr when I want.

But let there be no mistake.

Don't think that I've become
one of those big, soft tomcats,

one of those delicate cats that
set up shop on cushions and sofas.

I have neither a master nor a castle.
I'll always remain the cat
who was given the name Mephisto.